DRAGON MASTERS
LAND OF THE SPRING DRAGON

BY

TRACEY WEST

BRANCHES

SCHOLASTIC INC.

DRAGON MASTERS

Read All the Adventures

More books coming soon!

TABLE OF CONTENTS

THIS BOOK IS FOR ALL THE PIXIE TRICKERS

out there. You know who you are! And a big thank-you
to Cyrus Carella for suggesting that Fallyn be called a Spring Dragon.
He is a real wizard with words. — TW

Text copyright © 2019 by Tracey West
Interior illustrations copyright © 2019 Scholastic Inc.

Library of Congress Cataloging-in-Publication Data
Names: West, Tracey, 1965- author. Loveridge, Matt, illustrator. | West, Tracey, 1965- Dragon Masters ; 14.
Title: Land of the Spring Dragon / by Tracey West ; illustrated by Matt Loveridge.
Description: First edition. | New York, NY : Branches/Scholastic Inc., 2019. | Series: Dragon masters ; 14
Summary: The Dragon Masters have defeated the evil wizard Maldred, but not before the Kingdom
of Bracken was devastated by Naga, the earthquake dragon; now Drake and his dragon, Worm,
must appeal to the spring dragon, Fallyn, who is their only hope of restoring Bracken before its
people starve--but Fallyn lives deep inside a secret fairy world, and Drake must pass a series
of tricky tests before he can even make his appeal.
Identifiers: LCCN 2018053885 ISBN 9781338263749 (pbk.) ISBN 9781338263756 (hardcover)

Subjects: LCSH: Dragons—Juvenile fiction. | Magic—Juvenile fiction. | Wizards—Juvenile fiction. | Fairies—
Juvenile fiction. | Famines—Juvenile fiction. | CYAC: Dragons—Fiction. | Magic—Fiction. | Wizards—Fiction.
Fairies—Fiction. | Famines—Fiction.
Classification: LCC PZ7.W51937 Lan 2019 DDC 813.54 [Fic] —dc23 LC record available at
https://lccn.loc.gov/2018053885

10 9 8 7 6 5 4 3 2 1   19 20 21 22 23

Printed in China   62

First edition, September 2019
Illustrated by Matt Loveridge
Edited by Katie Carella
Book design by Sarah Dvojack

HOPE FOR BRACKEN

Drake couldn't stop thinking about what had happened to the Kingdom of Bracken. Images flashed through his mind: Tall trees snapped in half. Fields, once green with crops, now cracked and crumbled. Wood from broken houses scattered across the dirt.

A few hours before, an earthquake had struck. An evil wizard named Maldred had controlled a powerful dragon called the Naga. He'd ordered the Naga to attack Bracken.

Drake and a team of Dragon Masters had stopped Maldred, but not in time to save Bracken. The earthquake had destroyed the crops. That meant the whole kingdom could go hungry.

We need to fix our land, Drake thought. *I will do whatever it takes.*

"Drake, are you listening?" asked Griffith, the king's wizard.

"Sorry, Griffith," Drake said, coming out of his thoughts.

Drake and two other Dragon Masters — Petra and Rori — were with Griffith in his workshop in the bottom of King Roland's castle. Petra was reading aloud from a book.

"Continue, Petra," Griffith said. "Everyone, listen closely. We may have found a way to rebuild Bracken."

Petra nodded, her blond curls bouncing. "Every year, when winter ends, the Spring Dragon brings spring back to the land of Inis Banba," she read from the book. "This dragon is connected to nature. She makes plants grow."

"That's perfect!" Rori said. "Maybe this Spring Dragon can make the crops in our kingdom grow back."

"We will have to go to Inis Banba and ask the Spring Dragon for her help," Drake said.

"Finding this dragon might not be easy," Petra said. "The book says she lives in a world hidden inside Inis Banba. The only one who can enter this world and find the dragon is her Dragon Master."

"Then we shall find the Dragon Master!" Griffith said. The wizard opened a box carved with pictures of dragons. The large green Dragon Stone glittered inside.

Griffith waved his hand over the stone.

"Show me the Dragon Master of the Spring Dragon," he said.

The Dragon Stone began to glow. Green light shot out of it.

I wonder what this new Dragon Master will be like? Drake thought.

A picture appeared inside the light. A girl with curly red hair and freckles stood in a field of wildflowers, next to a stone well. Her green eyes looked through wire spectacles. And like the other Dragon Masters, she wore a piece of the Dragon Stone around her neck.

"We found her!" Drake cried.

A NEW DRAGON MASTER

The red-haired girl's eyes narrowed. "Who said that?" she asked.

Petra gasped. "She heard us!"

Drake had seen the Dragon Stone work before. You could see and hear the Dragon Master inside the green beam of light. But the Dragon Master usually couldn't see or hear you.

Griffith's eyes widened. "This is very unusual! The well must be some kind of portal," he muttered, stroking his long, white beard.

The girl looked into the well. "I can see you in the water," she said. "I see one skinny wizard and three Dragon Masters. Why are you spying on me?"

"We aren't spying on you," Drake replied. "We need your help. Our kingdom was hit by an earthquake. It destroyed our crops."

"We read that the Spring Dragon can make plants grow," Petra added.

"Can you bring her here to fix our crops?" Rori asked.

The girl's eyes twinkled. "Do people in your land not know the word *please*?" she asked.

"*Please*, can you help us?" Drake asked.

"That is not up to me," she said. "That is up to Fallyn."

"Is that your dragon's name?" Petra asked.

The girl nodded. "Yes. And I am Breen," she answered. "I am Fallyn's dragon master, but Fallyn is not like other dragons. She belongs to *everyone* who lives in Inis Banba. Even though I am her master, I cannot command her to leave this land. She must decide that on her own."

Just then, Breen's Dragon Stone glowed green, and she shut her eyes. Drake knew that she was hearing her dragon's voice inside her head.

"Fallyn says that she will see one brave Dragon Master," she said.

Rori frowned. "Just one?"

"Very few humans are allowed in Fallyn's hidden world," Breen answered.

"Drake shall go," Griffith said. "His Earth Dragon, Worm, can transport there in a flash. There is no time to waste."

"You'll find me in Mave's Meadow," Breen said. Then the green light faded.

Drake's stomach fluttered. He and Worm had traveled to faraway lands before. But Drake had always had at least one friend with him.

Petra touched Drake's arm. "Don't worry, Drake. You can do this," she said.

Rori smiled. "Go bring us that dragon and save Bracken!"

"I won't let you down!" Drake promised.

Drake left the wizard's workshop. Worm was waiting for him.

"We need to go to Inis Banba right away," he told his dragon, "to meet a Dragon Master named Breen in a place called Mave's Meadow. Can you get us there?"

Worm nodded, and Drake put his hand on Worm's scales.

"Let's go!" Drake cried. He closed his eyes as a bright green light flashed.

THE TEST

When the light faded, Drake opened his eyes. Worm had transported them to a field of wildflowers. Breen stood by the well that the Dragon Stone had shown them.

Breen walked over to Drake and his dragon. She looked up at Worm.

"Hello, Worm," she said. "That's an unusual name for a dragon, isn't it? But I can see why Drake named you that." Then she turned to Drake. "Hello, Drake," she said. "Glad to meet you."

"Glad to meet you, too," Drake said. "It's nice that you and your dragon are going to help us."

"Now don't get ahead of yourself," Breen said. "Before Fallyn will agree to help you, you must find her."

"Can't you just take me to her?" Drake asked.

Breen grinned. "That would be too easy," she said. "To find Fallyn, you'll have to use your courage and your wits. And you'll have to leave Worm behind."

Drake's mouth dropped open. "What?" he asked. "Why?"

"You need to do this on your own, Drake," Breen replied. "Besides, there is only room for one dragon in the fairy world."

Drake's Dragon Stone began to glow. He looked at Worm.

I wasn't expecting this, Worm! Drake said inside his head.

You will be fine, Worm promised him. *I'll be here when you return.*

Drake turned to Breen. "Okay, I'm ready. I just hope it doesn't take too long to find Fallyn. We need to get back to Bracken soon."

"How long it takes depends on you," Breen told him. "I can get you started, but the rest is up to you. Now, let the challenge begin!"

Breen skipped across the field, whistling a tune.

THE FAIRY MOUND

rake followed Breen to a small, grassy hill.

"This is a fairy mound," Breen explained.

"I have heard of that," Drake said. "My mother used to tell me stories about a secret fairy world. She said the fairy mound was the way to get in. But I never believed her stories were true."

Breen smiled. "I bet you didn't believe in dragons, either, until you saw one."

Drake smiled back. "No, I guess I didn't."

"There are many different kinds of fairies in this secret world," Breen told him.

She touched her Dragon Stone, and it glowed. Then a hole opened up in the hill.

Breen stepped inside, and Drake followed her. They passed through a dark tunnel that opened up into a field of flowers. This place looked almost like where they had just come from. But Drake could see that it was different. The sky was a strange shade of pink, instead of bright blue. The colors on the flowers looked brighter.

"Welcome to the fairy world! It is similar to our world, but quite a bit different," Breen said. "You'll see. Come this way."

Drake followed Breen down a path through the meadow. Breen stopped at the start of a forest. The path split in two different directions.

"Which way do we go?" Drake asked.

Breen stepped to the side. "That is up to you, Drake."

Drake looked down the two paths. They both led into the woods.

How do I know which path will lead us to Fallyn? he wondered.

"Make up your mind, Drake," Breen said in a teasing voice. "Hurry now. Which will it be?"

Drake took a deep breath. Suddenly, he heard voices behind them. He turned to see a group of tiny men — none of them higher than Drake's knees — marching toward them. Each one had a white beard and wore a green shirt, green pants, and a pointy red cap.

"Here we go marching on and on, here and there and over and yon," they sang.

Drake's eyes got wide. "Who are they?" he asked Breen.

"Those fairies are called redcaps," she explained. "They like marching around a lot."

The redcaps marched toward Drake and Breen without glancing at them. When they reached the fork in the road, they marched down the path on the right. Then they stopped. All at once, they turned to face Drake.

"Follow us!" they cried.

THE REDCAPS

I think these fairies want to help me! Drake thought. He was about to take a step toward the redcaps when he stopped and turned to Breen.

"I guess you won't tell me if we should follow them or not," he said.

"No. I can't," Breen said. "That would be cheating!"

"But can you tell me something about them?" Drake asked.

Breen twirled her finger around one of her curls. "I guess so. What do you want to know?"

"Well, what kind of fairies are they?" Drake asked. "Are they nice?"

"They mostly like to march around," she answered. "But they do also like to have fun with humans who visit here."

"Hmm," Drake said. "What kind of fun?"

"You are asking too many questions, Drake," Breen said. "Choose a path!"

The redcaps had already begun to march away. "Wait for us!" Drake called out. He ran to catch up to the fairies. Breen followed him.

The redcaps marched into the woods.

"Here we go marching on and on, here and there and over and yon," they repeated.

They marched and marched. Drake kept expecting to reach the end of the woods, but they never did.

"I think we're going in circles!" he said.

"You are right," Breen agreed. She pointed to a tree with a twisted trunk. "We have passed by this same tree three times."

"Here we go marching on and on, here and there and over and yon," sang the redcaps.

Drake frowned. "I guess we shouldn't have followed them," he said. "Let's go back to the other path."

Drake tried to turn around — but he couldn't! His body swung forward and kept marching behind the redcaps. His legs were moving all on their own!

"Hey!" Drake yelled.

Are the redcaps using some kind of fairy magic? he wondered.

Drake couldn't slow down or change direction. Behind him, Breen was marching, too. They couldn't stop!

Drake made his legs move faster. He caught up to the redcap at the end of the line and tapped him on the shoulder.

"Excuse me," he said. "But we would like to stop following you now, please. We need to find Fallyn and save my kingdom."

The redcaps stopped marching. They all turned around and looked at Drake.

"But you must keep following us!" said one.

"We're having too much fun!" said another.

"Yes," said a third. "Going round and round is such a good time."

"I'm sorry, but I don't have time for games," Drake said. "My kingdom needs help."

"Sorry," one of them said. "We can't let you go."

"You have to let us go sometime," Drake said. "How long do you want to keep playing for, anyway?"

The redcaps all answered him at once.

"Forever!"

A TRICK

The fairies smiled up at Drake.

"You want me to march with you *forever*? You can't make me do that!" Drake said. His legs were still moving, marching in place.

"Yes, we can!" one of the redcaps said cheerfully. Then they all spun around and began to march again. Drake's legs followed them.

"Here we go marching on and on, here and there and over and yon."

Drake looked at Breen. "You could have warned me about the redcaps!" he said.

"I did," she replied. "I told you they liked to have fun."

"This isn't fun," Drake complained.

Breen shrugged. "It's fun for them."

Drake marched along the path, thinking. *I need to find a way to get the redcaps to let us go. But all I know about them is that they like to have fun.*

Fun... Drake repeated the word in his mind. Back home, the younger kids always wanted to pull him away from the field to play games. Games like sticks and stones, hop and skip, hide-and-seek...

Drake tapped the nearest redcap again, and the fairies all stopped marching.

"What is it?" the redcap asked.

"I know a game we can play," he said. "It's more fun than marching."

The redcap's eyes lit up. "More fun! What is it called?"

"It's called hide-and-seek," Drake replied. "You close your eyes and count. Breen and I will hide. When you open them, you have to find us."

"Ooh, that does sound like fun," said the redcap. "What happens after we find you?"

"Then it's *your* turn to hide," Drake said.

The redcaps all huddled together. They whispered to one another. Then they turned back to Drake.

"We will play your game!" they said at once.

"Great!" Drake said. "First, you have to release your magical hold on us, so we can hide properly."

"Done," the redcaps said, snapping their fingers.

Drake tested it. He turned and took a step.

My idea is working! he thought.

He turned back to the redcaps. "Perfect!"

One of the redcaps nodded. "Now we close our eyes and count, right?"

"Yes," Drake said.

The redcaps all closed their eyes. One redcap opened his. "How high do we count?"

"Ten thousand, six hundred, and twenty-three," Drake replied.

"Okay!" the redcap said, and he closed his eyes.

Then all the fairies began to count. "One, two, three..."

Drake motioned for Breen to follow him. They hurried back to the fork in the path, away from the redcaps.

HINKY PINK!

ou tricked the redcaps!" Breen said, giggling. "Those fairies will be busy counting all day. Nicely done!"

Drake smiled. "Thanks," he said. They had reached the fork in the path. "Let's try this way now."

They took the path on the left this time and quickly reached the edge of the woods. The path continued across another green meadow.

As they walked, a thick fog began to rise.

Soon, it was so thick that Drake could not see Breen standing right beside him!

"Is it always this foggy here?" Drake asked.

"Not always," Breen answered. "The fog rolls in when Hinky Pink visits the fairy world."

"Who is Hinky Pink?" Drake asked.

Then a voice came through the fog ahead of them: "Fog, fog, beautiful fog! It's great in a field or a hole or a bog."

"That's Hinky Pink," Breen whispered.

Drake strained to see the fairy through the fog. But all he saw was a faint light in the distance.

"Hinky Pink! Did you bring this fog?" Drake called out.

"This fog is mine, I will not lie! I've taken the clouds down from the sky," the fairy answered.

"I can't see which way to walk," Drake said. "And I need to find the Spring Dragon in a hurry. Can you please make this fog go away?"

"I'm happy when it's dark as night. My lantern is my only light!" Hinky Pink replied. "But if this fog makes you uptight, you can chase it away with something bright!"

Drake grunted. *This will not be easy*, he thought. *Where can I find a bright light?*

Then Drake looked down at his Dragon Stone and got an idea.

He turned to Breen. "Is it cheating if I ask Worm for some help?"

"I think it is fine as long as he doesn't transport here," she replied.

Drake's Dragon Stone glowed green as he contacted Worm.

Worm, can you hear me? Drake asked.

He heard his dragon's voice in his head. *Yes.*

There is a fairy making a fog down here. Can you make my Dragon Stone bright enough to burn away the fog? Drake asked.

I think so, Worm replied.

Drake's Dragon Stone began to glow brighter . . . and brighter . . . and brighter . . . Drake could see Breen now. And up ahead, he could make out a strange little man! The man was about Drake's height and wore funny striped pants. He held a lantern in one hand.

Hinky Pink stomped his foot. "Oh, drat! You've won! Now here comes the sun!" he cried.

Hinky Pink and the fog both vanished.

Drake blinked in the bright sunlight. He could clearly see the path. And up ahead, he saw something new: a boy. A boy with black hair and a Dragon Stone around his neck.

"Bo!" Drake cried.

A FRIEND APPEARS

rake was surprised to see his best friend in this magical land.

"How did you get here, Bo?" Drake asked. "Did Griffith send you?"

"Hurry, Drake!" Bo replied, ignoring his question. "I know how to find Fallyn. Follow me!"

Drake took a step forward, but stopped. *Something doesn't feel right*, he thought.

"Hurry, Drake!" Bo urged.

Drake looked at
Breen. "Bo is my
best friend. But it
doesn't make sense
for him to be here,"
Drake said. "Is this
really him?"

"You know I can't
help you on this
journey," Breen said.

"Think, Drake. If Bo is your best friend, you
should know if it is him."

"Drake, come on!" Bo cried. "It's me. It's
really me!"

This boy looks like Bo, Drake thought.
*But maybe it's a trick. Hema, the Gold Dragon,
could change her shape into any form. Maybe
this is a fairy pretending to be Bo.*

"Bo, I am not sure if it's really you,"
Drake said.

Bo frowned. "Of course it's me, Drake. I'm your best friend!"

Bo knows me better than anyone, Drake thought. *If this is a fairy and not Bo, then maybe a trick would show me the truth.*

"We always stick together," Bo said.

"You're right . . ." Drake answered slowly. "Like that time you and I went to Maldred's workshop with Darma and the Gold Dragon."

"Exactly," Bo said. "That was a pretty scary adventure."

Drake stepped forward. "Aha!" he yelled. "Now I *know* you are not Bo because Bo didn't go with me to Maldred's workshop. Rori did!"

The boy's eyes flashed with blue light. "No fair! You tricked me!" he said. Then his whole body began to glow.

The boy transformed into a shining blue horse with glowing eyes!

Startled, Drake jumped back and fell to the ground.

The horse reared up on its hind legs. It
whinnied and then ran away.

THE SPOOKY FOREST

"Congratulations!" Breen said, helping Drake to his feet. "You tricked the pooka!"

"What's a pooka?" Drake asked.

"A pooka is a fairy creature that can take any shape," Breen replied. "It usually takes on animal forms, like that horse."

Drake sighed. "I wish you were allowed to help me find Fallyn. I guess you can't tell me if we're getting close?"

Breen shook her head.

"I didn't think so," he said. "I just hope we find her soon."

Drake marched along the path to the edge of a second forest. The needles on the tall pine trees were so dark that they looked black. The trees had black trunks.

Drake gulped. "This forest looks pretty scary," he said. "Is it safe to go in here?"

"You have to decide for yourself, Drake," Breen said.

Drake nodded. He looked up at the tall trees and took a deep breath. "Okay. Let's go."

As soon as he set foot in the dark forest, Drake felt a chill. He shivered. An eerie hush fell over them as they made their way through the trees. The earth felt soft and squishy beneath Drake's feet.

Behind him, Breen began to sing in a sweet voice.

"The blackbird was a fine-looking fellow. His feathers were black and his bill was yellow. He flew over the field and over the trees. He soared and he swooped on the soft spring breeze."

The song made Drake feel a bit less scared. "That's a nice song, Breen. Where did you —"

He turned and looked back. But Breen was gone.

"Breen?" Drake asked. He turned in a circle, looking for her. His voice got louder. "Breen! Breen!" His voice echoed against the trees.

He was all alone.

Drake had never been alone on a mission before. Other Dragon Masters had always gone with him. So had Worm. He thought of Worm waiting for him by the fairy mound outside the fairy world. *I wish Worm were by my side right now*, he thought.

Drake gazed at the dark woods all around him. *Is Breen playing a trick on me?* he wondered. *Or is she in trouble? I should try to contact Worm...*

But before he could, small fairies floated out of the trees toward him. Their clothes were the color of tree bark, their hair looked like moss, and their wings were tree leaves.

They quickly surrounded him!

THE RIDDLE

The tiny fairies closed in around Drake.

"Who has entered our forest?" one of the creatures asked.

"My name is Drake," Drake replied.

"My name is Kiora, and we are the wood sprites," the fairy said. "What are you doing here?"

"I am on my way to see the Spring Dragon," Drake explained. "I need her help. Her Dragon Master, Breen, brought me here. But Breen just disappeared. Can you help me find her?"

The wood sprites grouped together and talked in low voices. Then Kiora flew in front of Drake's face.

"We can help you," she said. "But first, you must pass a test."

"There sure are a lot of tests in the fairy world," Drake mumbled.

Kiora put her hands on her hips. "We can go away, you know. Do you want to find the Dragon Master or not?"

"Yes, I do!" Drake said quickly. "What is the test?"

"You must find a flower in the forest and bring it to us," Kiora answered.

"Any flower?" he asked.

Kiora shook her head. "No. One special flower. Listen."

The wood sprites began to chant at once.
"Find a flower the color of the sky.
With a cherry for an eye.
It has more petals than the legs of a horse.
But fewer than a spider's legs, of course!"

Drake tried to remember all the clues. *Color of the sky. Cherry for an eye. More than four petals. Fewer than eight petals.*

"I'll find it," Drake promised.

Drake jogged through the forest, followed by Kiora. He looked around for flowers, but he couldn't imagine finding any in this dark, spooky place.

Flowers need sunlight to grow, Drake thought. *I need to find a brighter area in this forest...*

Soon he came to a clearing in the woods where colorful flowers bloomed.

Drake ran to a patch of blue flowers and knelt down. "Color of the sky," he said. "And look, they have bright red centers. Just like cherries. These must be the flowers in the riddle! Now I just have to count the petals."

One, two, three, four, five, six, he counted to himself. "This is it! Six is more than four and less than eight. That was easy!"

"But that is not the right flower," Kiora said.

Drake frowned. "But it has a red center like a cherry. Six petals. And it's blue, the color of the sky."

"Is it?" Kiora asked.

"Of course the sky is —" Drake started to say, but then he looked up to see the pink sky overhead.

"Oh, I forgot," Drake said. "The sky in the fairy world is pink, not blue."

Kiora giggled. "Very good! Keep looking!"

Drake searched and searched until he found some pink flowers. They had red centers. He counted the petals.

"Four petals. That's not enough," he said, frowning. He counted the petals on another pink flower. "Nine petals. Too many!"

He counted the petals on flower after flower. Finally...

"One, two, three, four, five!" he called out. He plucked the flower from the ground and held it up to Kiora. "Is this it?"

"It is!" the fairy replied. "And now we will help you find the Dragon Master."

Kiora sprinkled glittery dust on the flower. It flew out of Drake's hand and planted itself back in the ground. Then it began to grow... and grow ... and grow. The flower grew bigger than Drake.

"Whoa!" Drake exclaimed.

Then the flower stem bent toward Drake. The petals surrounded him, and the flower swallowed him up!

"Good luck finding your friend!" Kiora called out.

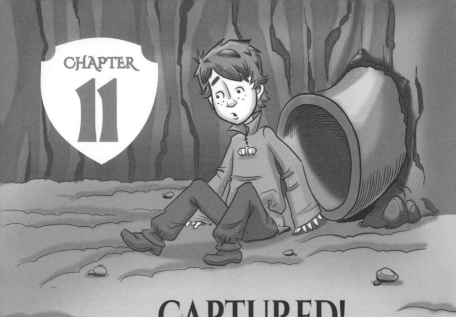

CAPTURED!

Drake tumbled down inside the enormous green tube of the flower stem. It spat him out on the dirt.

Drake stood up and looked around. He was underground. As his eyes adjusted to the dim light, he heard a voice.

"Drake! Over here!"

Drake ran toward the voice and discovered Breen behind metal bars, trapped in a cave.

"Breen, I'm so glad I found you!" he yelled. He grabbed the bars and gave them a tug. They didn't budge. "What happened? Who put you in here?"

"It's terrible," Breen answered. "An evil ogre scooped me up and brought me here. He's coming back to eat me!"

"An ogre?" Drake asked. "You mean like a big, mean giant?"

Breen nodded. "Can you get me out of here, Drake?"

Drake studied the cave. He wouldn't be able to bend the thick metal bars. He did not see a way out. *What can I do?* he wondered.

Suddenly, the ground beneath his feet began to shake.

"The ogre is coming back!" Breen yelled.

"Fee, fi, fo, fum! I need food in my tum-tum!" the ogre chanted.

Drake turned to see an enormous creature with a big belly stomping toward them.

"Run, Drake! Save yourself!" Breen shouted. "If you get eaten, you'll never save your land. Go now!"

Breen's right — if I don't leave now, I may never find Fallyn, Drake thought. *But I can't leave her here to get eaten!*

He threw his body in front of the cave.

The ogre roared as he thumped toward Drake. *"Aaaaaaargh!"*

THE SPRING DRAGON

I can't let the ogre hurt you, Breen!" Drake yelled.

He bravely faced the ogre.

"If you want Breen, you'll have to go through me!" he called out.

The ogre stomped up to Drake. Drake could feel the monster's hot breath on his face.

"Stay back!" Drake warned, balling his hands into fists.

The ogre ignored Drake. He moved past him and pulled apart the bars on the cave with his strong arms. Breen calmly stepped through the opening.

"Thanks, Blorp," Breen said.

"Did I do a good pretending job?" Blorp asked.

Breen nodded. "The best."

Drake stared at them. "You mean, he's not dangerous?" Drake asked Breen.

"Blorp? No, he's a softie," Breen said. She waved to the ogre. "See you later!"

The ogre marched off.

"That was another trick?" Drake asked, but he wasn't angry with Breen. A wave of relief washed over him.

"Another *test* — and you passed!" Breen said. "You stayed to protect me when you could have run away to save yourself. Now Fallyn knows you can be trusted."

Drake's heart was still pounding. "That was a pretty scary test!"

"Fallyn has to be careful, Drake," Breen said. "There are greedy people in the world. People who would steal her and use her powers just for themselves. That is why she lives in secret. And why she will only help those who are worthy."

"So, does that mean I get to see Fallyn now?" Drake asked.

Breen grinned. "Follow me."

She led him out of the cave.

Breen led Drake into a bright meadow. A beautiful green dragon sat on a hill covered with flowers. Her wings looked like big leaves, and tiny leaves sprouted from her body.

"Fallyn, we made it!" Breen said.

Her Dragon Stone began to glow. Breen smiled.

"Fallyn says that you have been very brave and smart, Drake," she said. "She will help you."

"Thank you, Fallyn," Drake said. "Can we go see my dragon, Worm? He can take us to Bracken right away."

Breen climbed onto Fallyn's back.

"Come on, Drake," she said, helping him up.

The Spring Dragon flapped her wings and flew into the air. They soared over the forests and meadows.

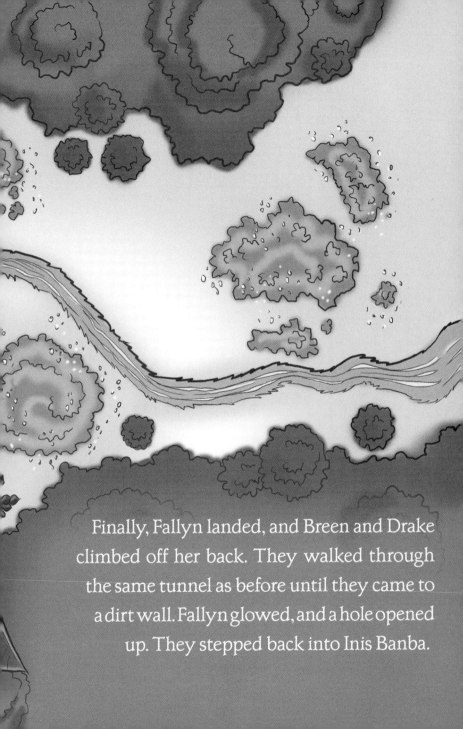

Finally, Fallyn landed, and Breen and Drake climbed off her back. They walked through the same tunnel as before until they came to a dirt wall. Fallyn glowed, and a hole opened up. They stepped back into Inis Banba.

Worm was waiting for them. *I knew you would find Fallyn*, he told Drake. *Good job!*

"Thanks, Worm," Drake said.

He held out his hand to Breen.

"Touch Fallyn, and then I'll touch Worm," he instructed. "Once we're all connected, we can transport."

"I've never been outside Inis Banba before," Breen said. "This is exciting!"

She grabbed Drake's hand and put one hand on her dragon. Then Worm transported them all to Bracken in a burst of green light.

GREEN

Drake, Worm, Breen, and Fallyn landed in the fields of Bracken. Breen looked around at the cracked earth and withered crops.

"This will be a very big job for me and Fallyn," she said.

Curious villagers started to gather around them. Then Drake heard a familiar voice.

"Drake!"

He turned to see Bo running toward him. The other Dragon Masters — Rori, Ana, and Petra followed him, along with Griffith, the wizard. But Bo was running faster than any of them.

"Bo!" Drake cried. He ran up to Bo and hugged him. "It's really you!"

"What do you mean?" Bo asked. "Who else would I be?"

"That's a very long story," Drake said. "I'll tell you later. Right now, meet Breen and Fallyn the Spring Dragon. They're going to fix Bracken for us!"

Ana gazed at Fallyn with wide eyes. She turned to Breen. "Your dragon is beautiful!"

"Even more beautiful than I imagined," Petra said.

"She *is* beautiful," Rori agreed. "I hope she's powerful, too."

"Just you watch," Breen said. "Please stand back, everybody."

Everyone made a wide circle around Breen and Fallyn. Breen faced her dragon. Her Dragon Stone glowed.

"Fallyn, please bring the crops back to these fields," she said. "Beans, peas, oats, barley, wheat, potatoes, cabbages, carrots, parsnips, spinach..."

Breen stopped and looked at the Dragon Masters. "Am I forgetting anything?"

"Onions," Drake replied. "Don't forget the onions!"

"Flowers would be nice, too," Ana added.

Breen nodded. "And onions and flowers," she told Fallyn.

The dragon's body began to glow with a soft yellow-green light. She closed her eyes.

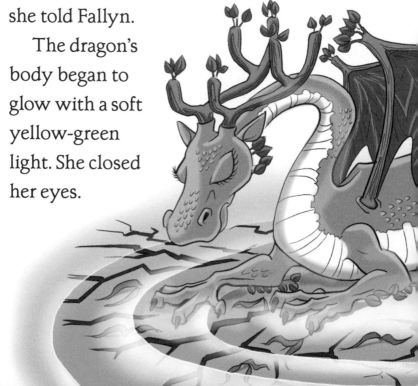

The light traveled through Fallyn's body, down to her feet, and then shot into the ground. The light spread across the brown, broken earth.

Fallyn is sending her energy into the land, Drake realized. He looked down at his feet and saw the dragon's light glowing beneath them.

He felt the dirt start to move — not shake, like in an earthquake. The cracks in the earth closed up. Then something began to gently push up from under the ground.

Breen twirled in a circle around her dragon. Breathless, they all watched as Fallyn's glow grew brighter and brighter.

THE DRAGON FLOWER

Slowly, tiny green shoots sprouted up from the dirt.

"It's working!" Drake cried. "Step off the fields to make room for the plants."

Everyone raced to the huts on the edge of the village. Then they watched the plants grow at amazing speed. They grew taller and taller with each second.

Soon, tall stalks of young green wheat waved in one spot. In another, the bushy green leaves of spinach appeared. Drake's heart leapt at the sight of skinny green onion tops, growing in neat rows.

Fallyn's glow slowly faded. Breen stopped spinning. The villagers stared, their mouths open, at the sight of the green crops. Nobody spoke for a moment.

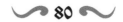

Then Rori yelled out, "Wow! That was amazing!"

The villagers let out a cheer. The Dragon Masters and Griffith ran out into the fields.

Breen was slumped up against Fallyn in a circle of yellow-and-red flowers. The dragon's ears were drooping.

"What do you think?" Breen asked, with a happy and proud smile on her face.

"I think that all those fairy tests were worth it," Drake said. "You saved a whole kingdom! Thank you. Thank you both."

"Yes, thank you," Griffith said. "You are one of the most powerful dragons I have ever seen, Fallyn. You both must be quite tired."

"Worm and I can transport you home," Drake offered.

"That would be very nice," Breen agreed. Her Dragon Stone glowed. "Fallyn says she was happy to help you all."

Drake and Worm quickly transported Breen and Fallyn back to Inis Banba.

"I'll miss you," Drake told Breen. "Even if you did trick me a lot."

She grinned. "Come back to Inis Banba anytime, Drake. We can play hide-and-seek for real!"

Then Drake and Worm returned to the fields of Bracken.

Ana looked closely at the yellow-and-red flowers.

"I've never seen flowers like these before," she said. "They look like dragons!"

Drake knelt down to get a better look.

"You're right," he remarked. "The flower looks like a dragon's head, with fire shooting out of it."

"And the petals look like spikes or horns," Petra added.

"Fascinating!" Griffith said.

"We should call it a Dragon Flower," Rori suggested.

Ana nodded. "That's perfect!"

Suddenly, they all heard the low rumble of thunder. Dark clouds appeared in the sky.

"A storm is coming!" Petra cried.

"Rain will be good for the crops," Bo said.

"I don't think it's a storm," Drake said.

"Look!" Rori cried.

Neru the Thunder Dragon flew across the sky!

A NEW MISSION

Neru swooped down toward them.

Petra's eyes widened. "Is the Thunder Dragon going to attack?" she asked.

"No," Griffith said. "His Dragon Master is not with him."

Rori gasped. "I almost forgot about Eko!"

Eko was Griffith's first student. She had run away with her dragon, Neru, a long time ago. Years later, she tried to free King Roland's dragons. She failed and was captured, but Rori helped her escape. Rori had even stayed with Eko for a while.

Neru landed next to Worm. The two dragons stared at each other for a moment. Then Drake heard Worm's voice in his head.

Neru is worried about Eko, Worm said. *He says she is missing.*

Drake turned to Griffith. "Rori and I last saw Eko in Maldred's workshop. Maldred used red dust to make her disappear!"

"We should have tried to find her. Or checked on Neru," Rori said. "But we've been too busy trying to save Bracken."

Griffith frowned. "What happened?"

"It's complicated," Drake said. "Eko was trying to help Maldred get control of the Naga."

"I'm not surprised that she was helping a dark wizard," Bo chimed in.

"Eko just wanted the Naga to be free," Drake explained.

"And in the end, she ended up helping us," Rori interrupted. "Maldred was going to feed us to the Naga. Eko tried to save us. That's when Maldred tossed magic dust on Eko, and she disappeared."

Griffith stroked his beard. "If that is the case, then we must help her."

Rori turned to Bo, Petra, and Ana. "We need to save her. Please?" she asked. "Drake and I owe her."

"Of course!" Ana said, and Bo and Petra nodded.

"Then it looks like we have our next mission," Drake said. "We have to find Eko!"

TRACEY WEST has written dozens of books for children. She once wrote a series about fairies called Pixie Tricks. Some of the creatures from that series made their way to Fallyn's magical fairy world.

Tracey is the stepmom to three grown-up kids. She shares her home with her husband, one cat, two dogs, and a bunch of chickens. They live in the misty mountains of New York state, where it is easy to imagine dragons roaming free in the green hills.

MATT LOVERIDGE loves illustrating children's books. When he's not painting or drawing, he likes hiking, biking, and drinking milk right from the carton. He lives in the mountains of Utah with his wife and kids, and their black dog named Blue.

DRAGON MASTERS
LAND OF THE SPRING DRAGON

Questions and Activities

An earthquake struck Bracken. Why do the Dragon Masters think a Spring Dragon could help rebuild the kingdom?

The redcaps use fairy magic on Drake. How does Drake trick them into releasing him?

Bo shows up in the fairy world. Is it *really* Bo? How does Drake test him?

Drake has to travel without Worm or his friends. When have YOU had to face something alone? How did you feel? Write about your experience.

Drake gets swallowed by a flower after a fairy sprinkles glittery dust on it. Imagine you sprinkle fairy dust on your favorite flower. What happens? Draw and label your magical plant!